Will You Be MY Friend?

Molly Potter

ILLUSTRATED BY Sarah Jennings

FEATHERSTONE
AN IMPRINT OF BLOOMSBURY
LONDON OXFORD NEW YORK NEW DELHI SYDNEY

For Karen, who is exceptionally good at being a friend.

Featherstone Education
An imprint of Bloomsbury Publishing Plc

50 Bedford Square
London
WC1B 3DP
UK

1385 Broadway
New York
NY 10018
USA

www.bloomsbury.com

Bloomsbury is a registered trade mark of Bloomsbury Publishing Plc

First published 2017

Text © Molly Potter 2017
Illustrations © Sarah Jennings 2017

British Library Cataloguing-in-Publication Data
A catalogue record for this book is available from the British Library.

ISBN: 978-1-4729-3271-6

Library of Congress Cataloging-in-Publication Data
A catalog record for this book is available from the Library of Congress.

5 7 9 10 8 6

Printed and bound in China by Leo Paper Products, Heshan, Guangdong

This book is produced using paper that is made from wood grown in managed, sustainable
forests. It is natural, renewable and recyclable. The logging and manufacturing processes
conform to the environmental regulations of the country of origin.

To view more of our titles please visit www.bloomsbury.com

Will you be my friend?

This book is all about friendship. It will help you understand what kind of friend you are, what to do if you ever fall out with your friends, and most importantly, what makes friends special.

Because everyone is different, no two friends are exactly the same. This is a good thing! You might have one friend who is very good at listening to you when you are upset, another who enjoys the same activities as you, and another who you find interesting to talk to. Each person's individual qualities make them unique.

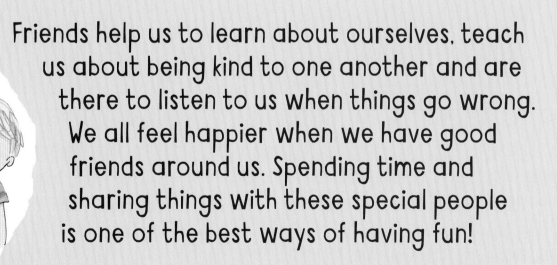

Friends help us to learn about ourselves, teach us about being kind to one another and are there to listen to us when things go wrong. We all feel happier when we have good friends around us. Spending time and sharing things with these special people is one of the best ways of having fun!

Contents

What is a friend?

How do I make friends?

What can friends do together?

What to do when a friend upsets you

What makes us a good friend?

What might make us a not-so-good friend?

How could you show a friend that you care?

Turn to page 18.

What do your friends think of you?

Turn to page 20.

What would your perfect friend be like?

Turn to page 22.

Nice things you could say to a friend

Turn to page 24.

How to help a friend who is upset

Turn to page 26.

Saying sorry to a friend

Turn to page 28.

What is a friend ?

A friend is someone who...

We enjoy spending time with.

We feel we can talk to about everything and anything.

We trust to keep our secrets.

We can be ourselves with.

Likes us just the way we are.

For you!

Often makes us feel good.

Enjoys talking to us.

Gives us a helping hand when we need it.

We feel like we can be ourselves with a really good friend. We look forward to seeing our friends and enjoy spending time with them.

How do I make friends?

Things we can do to help make friends...

Smile and look pleased to see someone.

Look at their face and make eye contact.

Let me show you the giant monster I made out of cardboard.

Find something you both like doing and talk about that.

I like your dress.

Say something nice to them.

Try to make them feel relaxed.

I was a bit scared about coming here too.

Ask questions to show you are interested.

Do you like cats or dogs better?

Go over and stand near to them.

Well he didn't bite!

DON'T decide anything about a person until you know them well.

She looks scary.

She's actually really nice.

We can sometimes feel a bit nervous about meeting new people but this feeling soon goes once we start talking to them. Remember they are probably feeling a bit nervous too.

9

What can friends do together?

With friends we can...

Play games together.

Chat about everyday things.

Do jobs that need doing together.

Make things together.

Give each other nice surprises.

Make each other laugh.

Teach each other about different things.

Just be together!

Doing something with a friend can make it more fun than if you do it on your own.

What to do when a friend upsets you

When a friend upsets you, you could...

Work out what it is exactly that you are upset about and explain it to your friend.

Make sure they listen to you and you listen to them.

Tell them how you are feeling because of what happened.

Help your friend understand that you want to feel better.

Say clearly what would make things better for you.

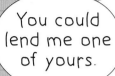

You could lend me one of yours.

Remember that everyone makes mistakes.

I didn't mean to be nasty, I was just feeling grumpy.

Forgive your friend when they say sorry.

Do something nice together when everything feels good again.

Whether they mean to or not, friends can sometimes upset us. When this happens, it's important to try and make things better again.

What makes us a good friend?

We are a good friend if we...

Forgive our friends when they make mistakes.

Show we care when they are upset.

Stick up for them if someone else is being nasty.

Take time to listen to them.

Ask questions to show we are interested.

Help them to solve problems.

Say nice things to them.

Show that we enjoy being with them.

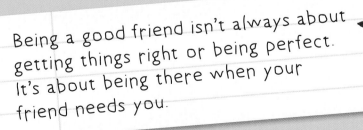

Being a good friend isn't always about getting things right or being perfect. It's about being there when your friend needs you.

What might make us a not-so-good friend?

We are not such a good friend if we...

Moan about our friend to someone else.

Are really bossy and tell our friends what to do all the time.

Tease them about how they look or what they say.

Interrupt them when they speak.

Tell them lies.

I have been to the moon actually.

Boast a lot.

I am definitely better at running, maths, art, writing and science than you.

Say we will do something for them and then don't do it.

But you said you would play with me.

Refuse to share things or take turns.

No, they're just for me to use.

There are ways of behaving that nearly always risk upsetting or annoying another person. It's a good idea to try and avoid these.

How could you show a friend that **you care?**

You could show your friend that you care by...

Greeting them with a smile that shows them you are really pleased to see them.

Spending time with them.

Noticing new things about them.

I love your new shoes.

Showing concern for how they feel.

Would you like to play with my pet tortoise?

Making them a card for their birthday.

Saying nice things about them.

Writing them a note that tells them how much you like having them as a friend.

Giving them a nice surprise.

Showing your friends that you care about them is a great thing to do. It can make your friends feel fantastic and it makes them see that you are lovely too.

19

What do your friends **think** of you?

Do you think they would say you...

Are good at sharing?

I can lend you my hat.

Are kind?

That's amazing!

Are good at giving compliments?

Can cheer them up and make them laugh?

Are good at listening?

Are fun to be with?

Are good at forgiving mistakes?

Always tell the truth?

Yes... I did copy you.

Sometimes we can be surprised when a friend tells us what they think about us but when they do we can always learn something about ourselves.

What would your **perfect** friend be like?

Would your perfect friend...

Be tidy or messy?

Be loud and lively or quiet and calm?

Be good at listening or talking?

Like doing the same things as you or have other interests?

Be unusual or ordinary?

Mess about a lot or be serious – or both?

Be good at sport, art, science,
maths or writing – or all of them?

Have lots of friends or
just have you as a friend?

There is probably no such thing as a perfect friend but we do tend to find ourselves drawn to some people more than others because we like how they are. Different people like different things.

Nice things you could say to a friend

You could say...

I love spending time with you.

See you in five minutes.

I look forward to seeing you again soon.

You often make me feel happy.

Would you like to play with me?

You are very kind.

I find what you say really interesting.

Thank you for listening to me.

You are a really good friend to me.

Nearly everyone likes to hear nice things said about themselves. You are more likely to get compliments if you give them to other people.

25

How to **help** a friend **who is upset**

When one of your friends is upset...

First check if they want
you to try and help.

Try and find out what
has happened.

Listen carefully to what they say.

Always take what they say seriously
– even if it seems silly to you.

26

Give your friend a hug if they want one.

Oops!

Ask your friend what would make things better.

I think we should all play together.

Help your friend if you can.

If you think you cannot help, find an adult who can.

When someone is upset, it's important to take it seriously and try hard to make them feel better.

Saying SORRY to a friend

When you say sorry to a friend it's important that...

You say clearly what it is
you are sorry about.

You don't say sorry in
a grumpy way.

You mean it!

You look at them and say
it in a serious way.

You want to make things better.

You will try never to do the thing you were sorry about again.

Let's not play near those bushes again.

You check they believe you are sorry.

Even if what happened was an accident, you say sorry for making someone upset.

Sorry.

When you have hurt or upset someone whether you meant to or not, it is important to say sorry. Sorry shows that you want to make everything better again because you care about the person you upset. Saying sorry to someone can speed up how quickly they feel better about what happened.

Friendships – a guide for parents

Why are friends important?

Humans are social animals and friends are important for your child's confidence, self esteem and well being. It is with friends that they learn important life lessons like sharing, negotiating, empathising, being considerate and listening to others. Interactions with friends also teach children about themselves and make them more self-aware.

Making friends

You can help your child to make friends by teaching them friendly behaviours like smiling, being polite, and asking questions to show you are interested. Outgoing children might have lots of friends that they spend time with. Quieter children will prefer to have fewer friends that they possibly form deeper friendships with. Neither one of these scenarios is better or worse than the other – it's just to do with our personalities.

When things go wrong

Most children experience friendship difficulties now and then. Most of the time they manage to sort these issues out by themselves and when they can, it's best not to get involved. However, the following 'lessons' can help your children develop and maintain better relationships.

- ### Empathy

    Encourage your child to put themselves in their friends' shoes when things go wrong. What do they think their friend will be feeling? If they find this too difficult, ask them to imagine a third person watching what happened (like a teacher or an aunt) and what they would say about the situation. Also ask your child to imagine what other children would think about how they behave – especially if they engage in some unattractive behaviours like being bossy, not sharing or being boastful.

- ### Aim to sort it out

    When things go wrong in relationships, explain that talking to the person can usually sort things out so that everyone can feel better again. Encourage your child to find out what needs to happen in order for everyone to feel better again.

- ### Use 'I messages'

    Encourage your child to explain how an action made them feel using 'I messages':

    > Not 'You made me angry.'

    > But, 'I felt angry when you did that.'

    Nobody can argue with how you feel and it is also a less confrontational way of speaking.

- ### A person is not just as good or bad as their last action.

    There is a tendency for some children to decide that a person is completely and simply 'bad' when that person has upset them. This can get in the way of children wanting to sort out the situation and 'make up'. When your child falls out with someone because of something they did, remind your child that they were friends not that long ago and that the action that has made them fall out is a temporary blip. Ask your child to think of some of the good times they have had in the past with the child they are having difficulties with. Hopefully this will help your child to want to make the effort to remedy the situation.

- ### Forgiveness

    Help your child to let go and forgive when other children have done something that upset them. If they cannot forgive, their friendship will continue to be affected.

• Fogging

There will be occasions when another child will say something nasty to your child. Teach them 'fogging' where the person being insulted goes along with what has been said. This takes all the power out of the insult and makes it less likely that the insult will happen again. For example:

Insult: 'You're rubbish at playing football.'

Response: 'Yes I know. Let's hope I get better huh?'

• Diversity

Help your child to understand that everyone is different and that they like different things, and that this is a positive thing. While it is good to have some things in common with a friend, it's also important to respect any differences.

When your child wants your help

If your child asks you for support with a friendship difficulty, start by simply listening and taking it seriously. It will be very real for your child however trivial it might seem to you. Next, you can help your child to feel better about whatever happened to cause upset by reducing the intensity of their feeling – using visualisation. Ask your child to recall what happened as if it was on the television.

Then ask them to:
• Change the picture to make it black and white.
• Turn the volume down.
• Recall the memory but with a funny tune playing over it this time.
• Turn the other person into an animal with a funny voice.

This will hopefully take the potency out of the negative emotion and therefore make a solution more attainable.

Role model

Navigating friendships can be hard for children, but if you demonstrate that you value friendships and are always prepared to 'work at them,' they will of course learn this from you. Think about the messages about relationships that your child receives from you.

Friendship Quiz

Have fun doing this 'true or false' quiz!

Friends should like exactly the same things as we like. True or false?

It's important to have lots of friends. True or false?

Sometimes friends upset us but if we talk things through we can usually make everyone feel better again. True or false?

It's really important that we never upset our friends. True or false?

You don't have to say sorry to a friend if what you did was an accident. True or false?

We nearly always look forward to seeing a good friend. True or false?

There are some ways of behaving that can make it more likely that we will upset our friends. True or false?

There are lots of things you can say to a friend to make them feel good. True or false?

We tend to enjoy different things about different friends. True or false?

We can learn about ourselves by listening to what our good friends say about us. True or false?

32